HOW SMUDGE CAME

Story by Nan Gregory   *Pictures by Ron Lightburn*

Red Deer College Press

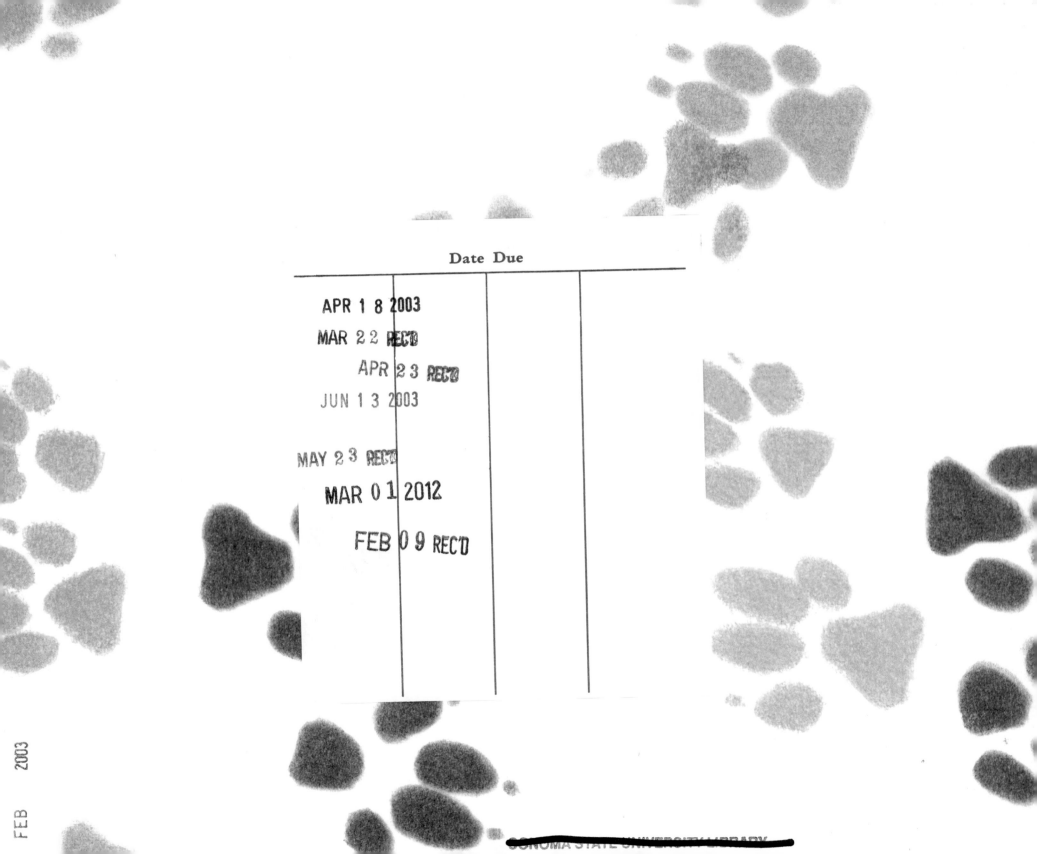

Date Due

APR 1 8 2003

MAR 2 2 REC'D

APR 2 3 REC'D

JUN 1 3 2003

MAY 2 3 REC'D

MAR 0 1 2012

FEB 0 9 REC'D

If there's one thing Cindy knows,
this is no place for a puppy.
    Up goes the puppy, tucked into her bag.
    Home goes Cindy.

If there's one thing Cindy knows,
it's don't let anyone see. Cindy
sneaks upstairs to her room.

"Is that you, Cindy?"
"Yes, Mrs. Watson."
"You're late. Dinner's getting cold."
"Right there, Mrs. Watson." Puppy goes under Cindy's bed.

At the big table, everyone is eating already.
Cindy fills her napkin with stew for the puppy.
  "No dessert, Cindy?"
  "No thanks." Her chair squeaks as she
pushes it back.

UP IN HER ROOM, PUPPY EATS HUNGRILY.

"Dear little puppy," croons Cindy. If there's one thing Cindy knows, this is her dog.

Knock! Knock! ON HER DOOR. "CINDY?"

Into the closet goes puppy.

The door opens. They never wait for her to answer.

"Cindy, John is drying the dishes. You can put away."

Cindy concentrates on the plates. *Don't break a plate, Cindy. Think about the plates, not the puppy.*

BACK IN HER ROOM, "OH, PUPPY, WHAT DID YOU DO?"
Cindy cleans up after the puppy.

Puppy sleeps under Cindy's covers. If there's one
thing Cindy knows, this is her best friend.

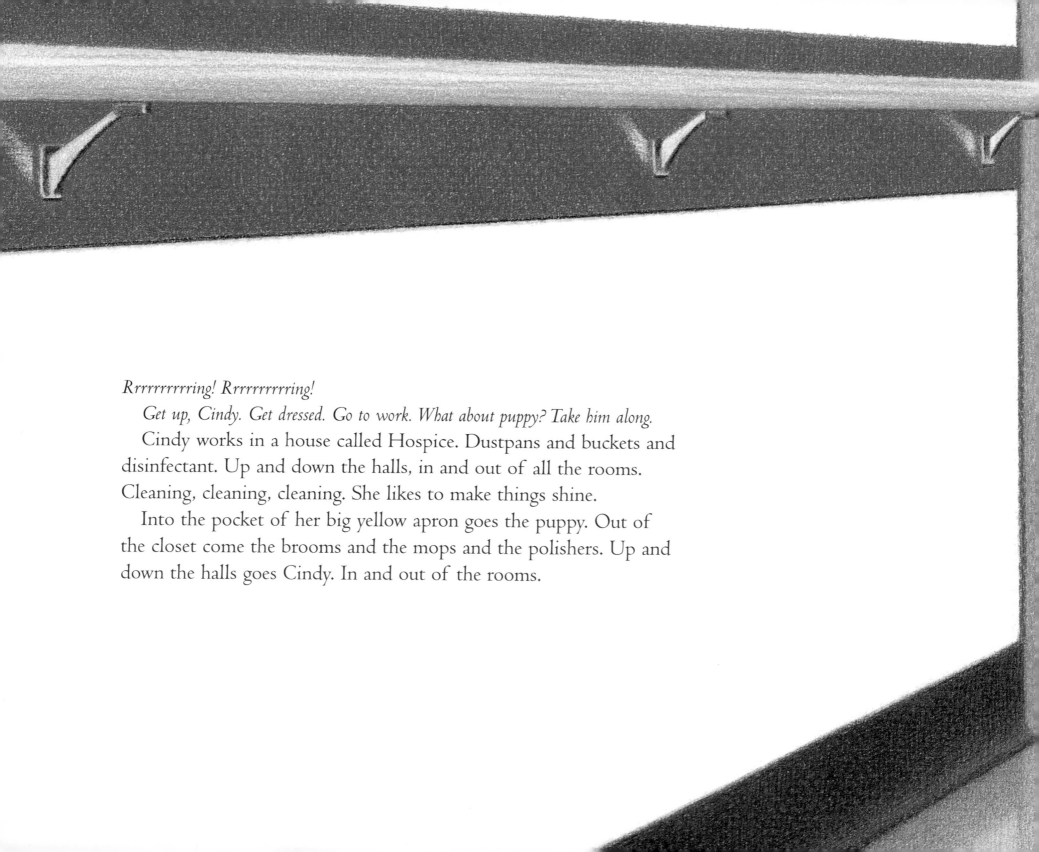

Rrrrrrrrring! Rrrrrrrrrring!

   Get up, Cindy. Get dressed. Go to work. What about puppy? Take him along.

   Cindy works in a house called Hospice. Dustpans and buckets and disinfectant. Up and down the halls, in and out of all the rooms. Cleaning, cleaning, cleaning. She likes to make things shine.

   Into the pocket of her big yellow apron goes the puppy. Out of the closet come the brooms and the mops and the polishers. Up and down the halls goes Cindy. In and out of the rooms.

Here's Jan, who isn't very old, but he is ugly with disease and he is going to die. Sometimes tears trickle out of his nearly blind eyes.

Clank!

"Is that you, Cindy?"

"Yup." In her apron pocket, the puppy whimpers.

"What's that sound, Cindy?"

"What sound?"

"Didn't you hear it?"

CINDY PUTS THE PUPPY ON JAN'S BED.
"Oh my, oh my. A puppy."
"Can you see him?"
"Not really. Just a smudge in the dark." Cindy smiles her slow smile.
"Same when I first saw him. Smudge-in-the-dark."

AT LUNCH, CINDY EATS HER SANDWICH ON THE BACK LAWN. SMUDGE EATS A BIT
of bread and sniffs around. Then back into the apron for the afternoon.

WHEN CINDY GETS HOME, PEOPLE ARE SHOUTING.
"Cindy, what's going on in your room? What
did you have in your room last night?"

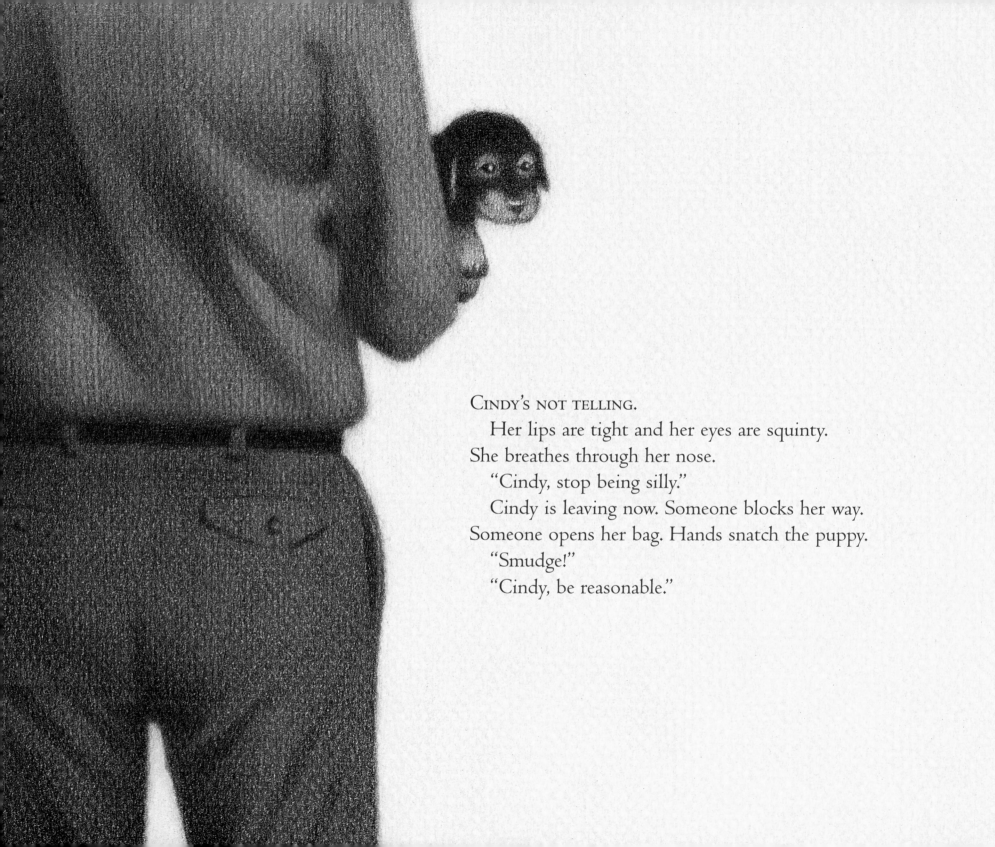

CINDY'S NOT TELLING.

Her lips are tight and her eyes are squinty.
She breathes through her nose.

"Cindy, stop being silly."

Cindy is leaving now. Someone blocks her way.
Someone opens her bag. Hands snatch the puppy.

"Smudge!"

"Cindy, be reasonable."

Now that they have the puppy,
everyone is reasonable.

"You can't have a puppy. You can't
take care of it. You work all day.
What would the puppy do all day
while you were at work?"

"Take him with me," Cindy says,
but they drown her with their words.
She tries to tune out. "SPCA," she
hears. "Good home." She will not
weep, but tears squeeze by. She starts
to hum.

"Go to your room, Cindy."

Next day, Jan props himself up.
   "Where's Smudge?"
   "'What would the puppy do all day?
You can't take care. You can't have a
puppy.'" Cindy is furious.
   Jan lies back.

After lunch, Cindy is back in Jan's room.

"What's SPCA?"

"A place that looks after animals until someone comes to take them."

"To a good home?"

"That's right."

Cindy snorts.

"Where is it?"

"I'm not sure. East side somewhere."

Cindy brings the phone book. "Find it. Please, Jan."

"Cindy, I can't see. I can't read the phone book."

"Who, then?"

"Carmen, maybe."

Cindy finds Carmen in the TV room. Carmen writes the address on a piece of paper. Cindy folds it carefully. It's far away, but Cindy has a bus pass. If there's one thing Cindy knows, it's how to get around.

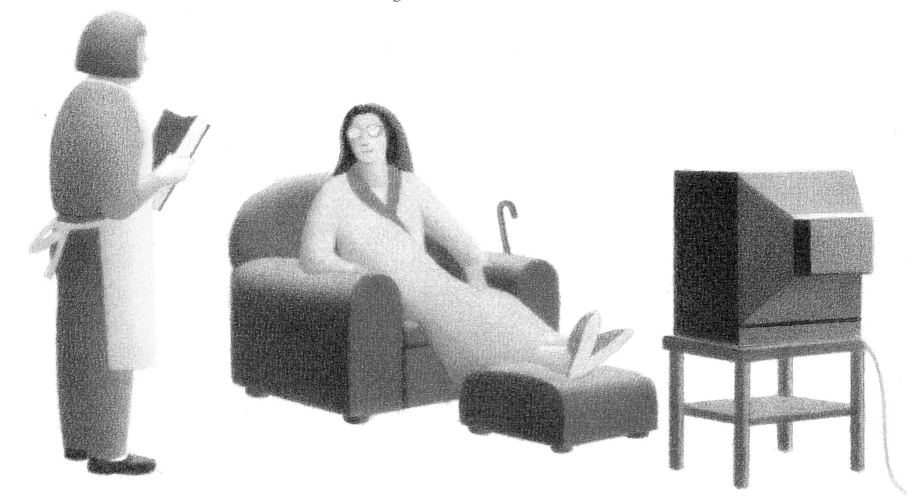

When a bus stops, Cindy shows the paper to the driver.
"Take the Number Nine all the way to Knight Street," the driver tells her. "Good luck."

SPCA keeps Smudge in a cage! The floor is hard and cold. He lies on papers!
"Good home!"
At closing time the clerk tells her, "Come back on Saturday at ten if you want the puppy."

"I'm getting Smudge on Saturday," she tells Jan.
"They give him away on Saturday."
    Saturday is chore day at the group home.
    "Cindy, what's wrong? You usually like to clean."
Dusting done, Cindy is gone like a leaf in the wind.

SHE IS PANTING AT THE DESK. "I'VE COME FOR MY DOG."

"Which dog is that?"

"My puppy. Small and black. Smudge."

"Sorry. All the puppies went this morning. Come back next week. We're sure to have more."

CINDY SITS IN THE PARK FOR A LONG TIME, BUT THE HURT WON'T STOP. Every time she breathes. If there's one thing Cindy doesn't know, it's how to find that puppy. *Crying won't help.*

Cindy makes a whistle with a blade of grass between her thumbs. "Here, Smudge! Here, Smudge!"

THERE'S NO PLACE TO GO BUT HOME.

"CINDY. THERE'S A PHONE MESSAGE."

What does Cindy care for messages? She lies on her bed and hums.

"Cindy, they want you at Hospice House first thing in the morning. You aren't in trouble, are you?"

At Hospice House, everyone is in the living room.

Jan is up. Jan never gets up. Carmen, too! *Is the TV broken? What's going on? Is there trouble?* If there's one thing Cindy doesn't need, it's another scolding. She starts to tune out.

"Cindy, we have something for you. Cindy, look."

Something soft is in her arms. Something cold nuzzles her chin. Cindy opens her eyes.

"Smudge!"

"We'll keep him here," says Jan. "For you, Cindy. For all of us."

If there's one thing Cindy knows, this is the perfect place for a puppy.

Northern Lights Books for Children are published by
Red Deer College Press
56 Avenue & 32 Street Box 5005
Red Deer Alberta Canada T4N 5H5

Edited for the Press by Tim Wynne-Jones
Designed by Limner Imagery Ltd. and Kunz + Associates
Printed and bound in Canada for Red Deer College Press

Financial support provided by the Alberta Foundation for the Arts, a beneficiary of the Lottery Fund of the Government of Alberta, and by the Canada Council, the Department of Canadian Heritage and Red Deer College.

COMMITTED TO THE DEVELOPMENT OF CULTURE AND THE ARTS

Canadian Cataloguing in Publication Data
Gregory, Nan.
How Smudge came
(Northern lights books for children)
ISBN 0-88995-143-8 (bound) —ISBN 0-88995-161-6 (pbk.)

I. Lightburn, Ron. II. Title. III. Series.
PS8563.R4438H68 1995   jC813'.54   C96-910461-5
PZ7.G73Ho 1995

The illustrations for this book were drawn on white Canson paper with Derwent coloured pencils.

In memory of Blitzen and Rex, and in hope of one more.
—Nan Gregory

In memory of Ethel and Heidi.
With thanks to the Victoria Hospice Society.
—Ron Lightburn